STORIES BY FIRELIGHT

For Edward with love

First published 1993

1 3 5 7 9 10 8 6 4 2

Copyright © Shirley Hughes 1993

Shirley Hughes has asserted
her right under the Copyright,
Designs and Patents Act, 1988 to
be identified as the author and
illustrator of this work

First published in the
United Kingdom in 1993 by
The Bodley Head Children's Books
Random House, 20 Vauxhall Bridge Road,
London SW1V 2SA

Random House UK Limited Reg. No. 954009

A CIP catalogue record
for this book is available from the
British Library

ISBN 0 370 31794 7

Printed in Hong Kong

STORIES BY FIRELIGHT

Shirley Hughes

The Bodley Head

London

Wild Weather

Winter is coming! The wind that blows
Hard from the north, from the land of snows,
Nips the fingers and reddens the nose
And strips the tree.

The track is sticky with mud and mire,
And crows string like crotchets along the wire,
And wanderers think of home and fire,
And so do we.

Sea Singing

Dᴵᴰ I tell you about the time I heard singing coming from the sea? It came very high and clear, from way out beyond the rocks under the cliff. I knew it wasn't the wind or seabirds calling. It was a woman's voice, I was sure of that.

'You mustn't go near the edge, not *ever*,' they had warned. 'It isn't summer, remember. The wind can be very strong.'

They were right, of course. They didn't need to tell me. I'm much too frightened of the rough sea, with those huge waves crashing up against the cliff and pouring and sucking over the boulders below.

I went looking in other places hoping I would hear it
again, all along the beach and over the rocks at low tide.
There wasn't much else to do anyway. My legs were still
thin and wobbly from being ill, but I walked and walked.
Sometimes I thought about my friends at home, doing
proper things like going to school and shopping and
watching their favourite programmes on television, and
how silly they'd think me wandering about on an empty
beach listening for voices.

When I told Mum's friend, Morag, about the singing, she didn't seem in the least surprised. She'd heard it herself, she said, but that was a long time ago.

I was staying with Morag, having a whole term off school. They said the sea air would do me good. Morag lives by the sea all the year round, not just for holidays. Her house is high up on the cliff. There's a room with a big window where she does her painting.

Late that afternoon Morag and I went for a walk along the cliffs. We didn't hear any singing, but the wind roared and the sky looked like a shoal of fish. Morag likes the sea best in winter.

In summertime, she told me, she has lots of visitors. They have picnics on the beach and boating parties and swim off the rocks. Morag's a very strong swimmer. 'Summer is fun,' she said, 'and it's a wonderful thing to have friends. But I'm always quite glad when they all go home and let me get on with my painting.'

Most of Morag's paintings are of the sea. Some of them she hangs up for everyone to look at. Some she stacks face up to the wall or leaves lying about on the floor. She doesn't much like people in the room with her when she's painting, but she doesn't mind me being there as long as I get on quietly with my own drawing.

Morag sings a lot while she paints. She sings along with the music on her tapes. When she's finished she washes her brushes and makes tea and then we talk. 'I expect it was a selkie you heard singing,' said Morag. Of course I didn't know what a selkie was, so she told me.

Selkies are seal people. They can cast off their skins and take human form. Once a fisherman saw a selkie playing and sporting on the rocks with her sisters and he stole her skin so she couldn't turn back into a seal again.

That night she came crying and moaning round his cottage all running wet with her black hair dripping, begging him to give back her skin. But he wouldn't, because he wanted her for his wife.

So she stayed and was a good wife to him. She cooked for him and cleaned the house and in time they had children, two boys and a girl. She seemed happy enough and sang at her work. But often she would carry the baby with her down to the shore.

She would stand there for a long time, looking out to sea. Then a big black seal would come and swim along quite close to the tide-line. And the baby would laugh and hold out her little arms to him.

The fisherman kept his wife's skin hidden away, always changing it to a different place so that she couldn't find it. But sometimes he would relent and let her hold it, just for a little while. One day, when she held it in her hands, she tricked him into thinking that something was wrong with the sheep on the hillside.

He hurried up there to see, but found nothing amiss. When he got back his wife was gone. The little boys were safe inside the cottage. They told him that their mother had taken the baby down to the sea. Panic stricken, he ran off down the cliff path, shouting her name into the wind.

He found his baby daughter playing happily on the shore. His wife's clothes were lying on a rock nearby. When he asked her where her mother was, she pointed out to sea. He picked her up and ran along the beach, calling and calling. But when darkness fell he gave up hope and went back to care for his family alone.

The selkie wife never came back to live with them again. But sometimes, in the morning, he would find wet footprints on the floor around the children's beds and their pillows damp with salt water. One night he lay in wait and the selkie appeared, crying over her children and kissing them as they lay asleep.

Then he lit the candle and told her how desperately he missed her and wanted her back. She replied sadly that she could never return. She told him that she had a seal-husband and other children in the sea, and that she belonged there with them.

That's really the end of the story. From that time on the fisherman just had to live wihout his selkie wife. Perhaps he had always half known that one day she would go back to the sea. But on the children's birthdays there were always presents — coral beads and combs and wonderful mother-of-pearl boxes — left on that same rock by the shore.

'How do you know all this about selkies?' I asked Morag
when she had finished the story.

She just smiled and said, 'My grandmother told me.'

Soon I was strong again and it was time for me to say
goodbye to Morag. She gave me one of her pictures to
take home with me.

It's very beautiful, all watery and curving. I have it on my bedroom wall.

Sometimes I think it looks like waves, or the shape of a seal, or perhaps a woman swimming. Sometimes, when I look at it for a long time, I think it looks like Morag herself, with her hair spreading like dark weed on the water.

Late Song

We glimpsed an old man in the late afternoon
(Rustling, shuffling, dry leaves scuffling)
In fading light with a sliver of moon
And the sun just going down.

He tramped past the wood by the side of the hill
(Nuts and berries, dark like cherries)
And where he walked it was suddenly chill
And the golden leaves turned brown.

And a brisk wind whipped through the shivering grass
(Sighing, moaning, branches groaning)
And stirred his beard as we saw him pass,
So nimble and yet so old.

But as his shadow was growing long
(Lean and lank in the chilly dank)
A robin whistled a last brave song
To herald the coming cold.

Mrs Toomly Stones

Cosy windows, closely curtained,
Colour TVs, glowing bright;
Our house looks like all the others,
But the one without the light
Is Mrs Toomly Stones'.

Other people say it's empty,
By the gate it says 'To Let',
But somewhere on the darkened landing,
Or in the hallway (you can bet)
Lurks Mrs Toomly Stones.

Behind the door the eyes are watching,
Sharp as cat and sly as fox,
Following me as I pass by there,
Eyes in the dead letterbox
Of Mrs Toomly Stones.

Who's that creeping in the bushes?
Moving in the tangled privet?
Peering through the dripping laurels –
Is it the neighbour's cat? Or is it –
Mrs Toomly Stones?

Can you glimpse a crouching figure
Somewhere by the shattered grate?
Did you see the curtain twitching?
Quickly! Hurry by the gate
Of Mrs Toomly Stones.

Other neighbours mend their motors,
Hang their washing when it's light,
Hurry off to school and office,
But the one who stalks at night
Is Mrs Toomly Stones.

If something moves on the veranda,
A shadow in the darkening street,
Run past the place and don't look back
In case you hear the padding feet
Of Mrs Toomly Stones.

In bed, listening to household noises,
Creaking boards and dripping taps –
Is that rattling at the window
Merely the wind? Or is it perhaps …
Mrs Toomly Stones?

A Midwinter Night's Dream

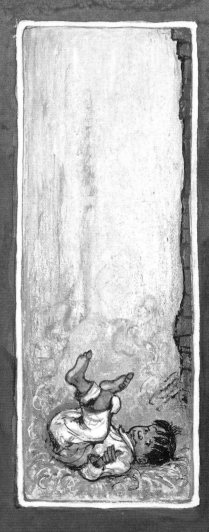

Inside the Inn

Who's that at the door?
It can't be a salesman at this time of night!
If it's someone collecting or scrounging for beer
Tell them we're busy and money's too tight.
There's so many around at this time of year;
I've given before…

What's that you say?
A couple requiring a meal and a bed?
We're completely full up and it's terribly late.
It's the wrong time of year, as I've already said;
I'd help if I could, with her in that state,
But I'm rushed off my feet and we're *so* understaffed,
So close it up do, there's a horrible draught,
And send them away…

First Light

And is it true that on that first dark morning
On the bleak hill, huddled among their sheep,
That shepherds, scratching themselves and yawning,
Drowsily chatting, longing for home and sleep,
Were the very first men on earth to know
That God had come to live with them below?

And was it perhaps the youngest, the boy, who was the first
To see the bright light radiant in the sky;
And, though it was winter, smelt the smell of flowers,
And caught a burst of heavenly music, floating far up high?
Then, touched by the brush of a golden wing,
Looked up to hear the angels sing?

Burning the Tree

William and Grandpa were taking down the tree. Christmas was over and it was time to put all the decorations away in the loft until next year. Grandpa pulled off the shiny glass balls and handed them to William who laid them carefully in their box. They took down the tinsel and unwound the fairy lights. Then they wrapped the two little glass birds and the angel with golden wings in tissue paper and put them away too.

When they had finished, the tree looked rather bald and old without its sparkle. The presents which had been stacked underneath its boughs had all been opened on Christmas day, of course. And it no longer smelt of that wonderful foresty green smell as it had when they bought it. It leaned sideways in its pot. A lot of needles came off and scattered on the carpet. 'What a mess!' said Mum. 'I'll never get them all up. You'd better move it out of the way, you two.' And she briskly plugged in the vacuum cleaner. Vacuuming always put her in a bossy mood.

William and Grandpa laid the Christmas tree in a dust sheet and dragged it as far as the back door, trying not to leave a trail of pine needles behind them. 'Get your coat. We'll have a bonfire,' said Grandpa.

William found his coat. Then he followed Grandpa to the door of his room and waited while he looked for his old gardening jacket.

Grandpa had not lived at William's house for very long, only since Gran had died. He had his own room and his own television set. It was quite a small room and it was very full of things.

There were some photographs on the mantel shelf –
one of Gran and Grandpa on their wedding day, one of
Mum when she was a baby and one of Grandpa's football
team. Grandpa was right in the middle, holding the ball,
because he was the goalkeeper. William spent a lot of
time in Grandpa's room. Sometimes they watched
television and sometimes they just chatted. William
loved hearing about all the adventures Grandpa had had
when he was a young man, and looking at his things.
There was one special box, a polished wooden one with
brass handles which stood on the high shelf above the
books. Grandpa never showed anyone what was in there.

But William had seen inside the box. He had peeped into it one day when Grandpa was out. He just couldn't resist the temptation.

It was a sad disappointment. There was nothing interesting to see, only some boring old letters, a train ticket, a few pressed flowers and some papers which looked like poems but the writing was too difficult for William to read. Afterwards William felt miserable and uncomfortable when he looked at the box. He felt bad about knowing what was in there when Grandpa didn't know he knew. He tried hard to forget all about it.

It was nearly dark when they went outside, with only a streak of red left in the sky. William and Grandpa dragged the tree down to the rubbish heap at the bottom of the garden. It was Grandpa's special place behind the greenhouse by the end wall. He spent a lot of time there, piling up leaves and garden rubbish. Then he would lean on his rake and light his pipe. Mum didn't like Grandpa to smoke indoors. She said she couldn't stand the smell.

They heaved the tree on to the big pile of leaves and twigs which was already there. Its bare arms stuck up bravely into the sky.

Grandpa went indoors again and fetched out a big bag full of old paper chains and the dry holly which had decorated the hall. He packed them round the tree. Then he pulled out his matches and set light to them.

'This will make a grand blaze,' he told William. The paper and holly caught at once and burned brightly. Then they glared into white ash and the twigs and leaves started to smoulder and crackle and give off smoke. Flames began to lick through them, small at first, creeping up towards the tree. When they reached the dry pine needles the whole thing suddenly took fire.

Flames shot up with great eddies of smoke. The Christmas tree branches were all at once bright and glowing, covered with festive sparks. As William watched, the wall behind seemed to melt and quiver. His eyes were watering, but the smell was wonderful. They stood and looked at the fire for a long time. They watched until at last the tree burned out and collapsed into the pits and caves of ash.

Then Mum called William indoors. He left Grandpa standing there, staring into the fire.

Later, when it was quite dark, Grandpa was still out there. They could see the red glow at the bottom of the garden.

'Supper will be ready in ten minutes,' said Mum, as she drew the curtains. 'Run and tell him, will you William?'

William put on his coat again and ran down the garden path. Grandpa was standing exactly where he had left him. But he had something under his arm. It was the box with brass handles.

'Let's have one more good blaze before bedtime,' said Grandpa as William joined him. And then he opened the box and flung all the papers and letters and things that were inside on to the bonfire. Just like that! They caught alight instantly, and once again the cheerful flames leapt up.

'But I thought they were special,' said William as they watched them burn.

'They were,' said Grandpa, 'but it's not things that are important really. The special things are in my head. And my heart. So why not get rid of the rest?'

William had never heard Grandpa say anything like that before. He didn't know quite how to answer. He took Grandpa's hand and stood leaning up against him until the flames died down and were finally gone.

'I looked into your box once,' said William.

'That's alright. You were welcome,' said Grandpa. 'They made a grand blaze, didn't they?' he added, after a pause.

William felt suddenly happy.

'Mum says I can stay up a bit and watch the football on television, as it's Saturday,' he told Grandpa. 'Will you watch it with me?'

'You bet I will!' said Grandpa. 'You run along and tell Mum I'll be in just as soon as I've finished this pipe.'

Coming Soon

Spring is coming! With promising patches
Of blue; and sunlight suddenly catches
A gleaming rooftop, where sparrows in batches
Flirt and flutter and pipe up snatches
Of hopeful song;

And windows are opened on stuffy rooms,
There's a shaking of mats and a flurry of brooms,
And it's light in the longer afternoons,
And boys on bikes whistle cheerful tunes.
It won't be long!

Morag's tale of the selkie wife in 'Sea Singing'
comes from a Gaelic myth, handed down for
centuries and many times re-told. Some of the
visual fantasies in 'A Midwinter Night's Dream' are
inspired by carvings on medieval buildings in
Bologna, Moissac, Sherborne, Verona, San
Quirico D'Orcia and many other places.   S.H.